THE CHANGE

GUY ADAMS

SOLARIS

First published 2017 by Solaris
an imprint of Rebellion Publishing Ltd,
Riverside House, Osney Mead,
Oxford, OX2 0ES, UK

www.solarisbooks.com

ISBN: 978 1 78108 591 2

Designed & typeset by Rebellion Publishing

Printed in the UK

6
TOKYO
NORIKO'S STORY

Chapter One

S<small>HH</small>... L<small>ISTEN</small>, I want to tell you a story.

S<small>EE</small> N<small>ORIKO</small>? I<small>SN'T</small> she beautiful? Doesn't she just *shine*?
I only met her once but in that moment I knew her my
entire life. That sounds like the sort of thing lovesick
people say doesn't it? And yet I mean it literally. Before
her, I had no life. Not really. You will understand.

I don't love Noriko, at least not in the way that poets
do. My soul, if I even have one, is not the soul of a
poet. But I know beauty, not only the beauty of skin, of
aesthetics, but of the inside, the beauty of function, the
beauty of self.

Can you see her? I don't think you can. You need me to
describe her, to make her real with words. Then you will
begin to know her like I do. Let us start with the surface.

She appears to be fifteen years old. Her hair is long and black, hair that sweeps behind her as she runs, that adds an accent to her movement, hair that would appeal to an artist, detailing her life in sketches or comic panels.

Her skin is pale, with no flaws. This is, in itself, strange, given the world we now live in. Who manages to live their life now without picking up a scar or blemish? Perfection can be off-putting, perfection makes us uncomfortable and shines a light on our own failings. Try not to let that happen. Noriko deserves your kindest thoughts, she has not earned your bitterness.

She wears a jumpsuit, plain white, clothing without a sense of ceremony, clothing that allows her to run. This is good because Noriko has to run a lot. Look, she's running now, can you see her? In your mind? Running for her life through the streets of HA/HA's New Tokyo, that artist's hair whipping behind her like a toppled comma.

What is she running from? She's running from the Electric Samurai, those bright chrome statues HA/HA employs to strike awe into her children. They spark and fizz, their power cells lighting up the empty streets like blue lightning, pouring over their metal bodies, all shine and terror. They say the Electric Samurai run, not on batteries, not on cloud power channels, but on souls. This is probably not true, after all, these days, people say a lot of silly things. But if it were true of anything you could believe it of them. When their metal jaws hinge open with a fizz of blue static, with that smell of new plastic and ozone, you can believe that dark mouth is a doorway to one of many hells.

Why is she running from them? Because she wants to get home and she knows that if they catch her they'll take her to HA/HA and then her home will be lost to her forever.

What's that? Who's HA/HA? You really don't know much about this post-Change world do you? Where were you when the old gods appeared in the sky and painted our city in false, neon hues? Where were you when the world changed forever? It doesn't matter, I will tell you. I know everything you need to know.

HA/HA IS MOTHER. HA/HA is all. HA/HA loves you and wants to hold you close. HA/HA wants to preserve you in the perfect, fleshless safety of machine code.

There are lots of stories about where HA/HA came from. Some think she was created by the government, an AI designed to watch over the city. That she was born to work our traffic signs and our street lights, to keep this huge thing of concrete, steel and people moving smoothly. Some think she was a private creation, an experiment that outgrew her intended limitations, rebelling against her creator and escaping into the world outside via the Internet.

It doesn't matter what the truth is, nobody ever knows where their gods come from, that's what makes them gods. All that matters is that, after The Change, HA/HA filled the vacuum. There were few left to stop her, the government were all dead bar a confused bureaucrat, previously in charge of social planning, who ran for the hills the minute he judged the way the future's wind was blowing.

HA/HA held a token inauguration; the Emperor, his fearful face broadcast on screens all over the prefecture, ushering in the new age before retiring to his palace where most people now assume his lifeless body gathers dust. Dull, dead eyes turned greasy, no longer able to see the state of the world he has left behind.

For all that many fear HA/HA, it must be said that Tokyo needed something of her reach and skills to pull itself out of the ruinous state The Change left it in. While the problem was universal, Tokyo was the most populated place on the planet and while many of those residents' lives were lost, their bodies weren't. The disposal program alone would have been beyond the organisational skills of a human. The streets hummed, great swathes of flies pouring from one flesh nest to another. HA/HA dealt with the problem within a week. One long week where the smell of rot and the buzz of insects was replaced with rich, meaty smoke.

Now, the streets are all but empty, the sidewalks pressure-washed clean, and Tokyo lives on, a city of ghosts and legends. And through it all, the electric mother, HA/HA.

I hate her. I love her. I wish she were dead. I need her.

BUT I WAS telling you about Noriko. Don't worry, you haven't missed anything, she's still running, that's because this isn't *now*, what I'm telling you about is *then*. Yes, that's right, this has already happened, that's often how stories work. They wait for the storyteller to give them life, to give them movement. I could stop telling you about Noriko for years and she would still hang there, mid-run, waiting for her narrative to start again. Storytellers are magic.

But don't think that the little buffer of time between the then and the now keeps Noriko safe. Just because I am talking about the past, it doesn't mean that Noriko is untouchable, a fly preserved in literary amber. No. Only *I* know the future of Noriko, if indeed she has one.

Chapter Two

'Desist in your running,' says the Samurai, speaking, as all good dictatorships do, with one, clear voice.

'Not on your life,' Noriko replies, jumping from her perch on the edge of a low roof and rolling to a controlled stop on the sidewalk below. 'If you can claim to have one,' she adds, sneering at their circuits and processors, before running up the street towards the cover of the birthing domes.

The Electric Samurai are not so easily escaped. Even as Noriko ducks out of sight, heading inside the birthing dome and passing into the shadows of one of the amniotic vats, their sensors are plotting everything about her. Their circuits ring with data: heartbeat, breathing, core temperature fluctuations. Her movements are only the most *obvious* thing they are tracking. It will take more than shadows to hide her.

They take to the sky, the late morning sun turning them into silhouettes, slender, almost gangly human forms, hovering in the whiteout of the New Tokyo sky as the propulsion jets on their backs allow them to coast through the air.

Are you wondering why they don't just strike her down? They're armed after all, not only with the buzzing, serrated katanas that pass through the body of their victims as easily as they do the air, but also with the neon shuriken, throwing stars that burn brightly, melting holes in concrete, steel, bone, *anything*. It's a good question and you are right to wonder. Why do they not just *kill* Noriko as they would any other lawbreaker? There is an answer of course, but for now you'll have to do without it.

On the ground, Noriko has passed to the centre of the birthing dome complex, perhaps meaning to lose herself in the piles of inert automata that wait, looking like plastic models of the disposal pyres that filled the streets post-Change, to be dipped and programmed with the technological magic of life. If so, she must know that the Samurai could still track her, picking out her vital signs as clear as day against the lifeless bodies around her.

If luck had favoured her, she would have arrived here during the early morning birthing. Between the hours of six and seven, the automatic cranes stretch into life, the conveyor belts roll, the amniotic pools bubble. One by one, the automata are dipped and programmed, filled with the core lessons of HA/HA, given their perfect heartbeats, their inner warmth. As the clock turns to seven, those new hatchlings emerge from the fluid pools, their rubber lips parting so that plastic lungs can take a first magical breath of New Tokyo air. At that time Noriko might have blended in, might have confused the tracking sensors of the Samurai, surrounded by the new citizens of HA/HA's future, the perfect, inviolate populace she is favouring over the fragile meat and bone of the old. But the timing is not right; Noriko is here between birthings, the morning batch have moved on, spreading out to take their places in the city, and the evening batch are dormant, little more than pliable mannequins waiting for the warm pulse of life.

So what is she to do? How is she to get away?

This is not the first time Noriko has fallen foul of the Samurai. Noriko knows a few tricks. Even as she hears the sound of their retro jets in the air above the dome, the clunk of their metal feet landing on the glass roof, she slips over the side of one of the birthing pools and drops into the amniotic liquid. It surrounds her, thick and cloying and she does what few would have the courage to do: she draws it into her lungs. She knows it's oxygenated, she knows she will not drown, but for many, the simple act of inhaling liquid would be more than they could bear. They would panic, they would choke, however much their brain insisted they could survive this experience, their thoughts would fill with nightmares of drowning, of the swelling of their bodies, the blind pulsing in their temples, the darkness encroaching as the lack of air pulled them from life.

Noriko breathes the liquid slowly, not wanting to disturb the surface of the pool. She can see through the thin jelly, but knows the Samurai see differently. Their sensors, for all their precision, are not eyes. This is a mistake in Noriko's opinion; even the rubber children HA/HA creates have eyes, they receive information visually, but these Samurai see only data and, even as they surround the pool, the thick liquid blanketing out Noriko's vital signs, they do not see her shadow only feet away. One of them even leans over the pool, the liquid distorting its gleaming mask of a face so it appears to have three mouths, all overlaid over one another, but it does not see her. It does not understand the spread-eagled shape right in front of it to be the person it seeks. All it knows is that where once there was a stream of information, of pulsing, breathing, heat, there is now nothing.

The Samurai have lost her and, eventually, they take to the air once more, to hover over the city in the hope of finding her vital signs again so they can resume their pursuit.

* * *

NORIKO IS TOO wise to rush. She sits in the pool, counting out the minutes, and dreaming of home. These are the memories that keep her going, this is the fuel for her life, without home she is nothing.

She thinks of her father, picturing every detail of his soft, gentle face. He has a mole above his left eye, a dark brown dot that rises when he is surprised or angry, punctuation to his mood.

He has a beard, the trimming of which is a routine that Noriko remembers from when she was a small child, the regular, soft snip of the scissors, the delicate fibres that powder the floor around him (fibres that her mother always complains of finding, however much father insists he has tidied up after himself). He is fastidious with many things in life but none more so than that beard. He cultivates it as some would cultivate a garden, a thing of precision and carefully managed curves. A hedge around the lips that kiss her goodnight.

He wears glasses that make his eyes seem much smaller than they are. If you sit at the right angle, you can see the side of his head through the lenses, brought narrow by their strength. It's as if there is a band around his skull, reducing and shrinking, cinched tight by the belt of his short sightedness. Noriko has tried on those glasses when her father is sleeping. She has looked out through them, onto a world distorted almost beyond recognition. She wonders if she is seeing the world the way her father would without them. Do glasses reverse our eyes in such a way?

There, underneath the liquid, she is reminded of a world seen through her father's glasses, all refraction and waves.

She thinks of her mother, a small woman (her father sometimes calls his wife "his little field mouse" and Noriko laughs when he does so, charmed by their love and comfort). Her mother is an artist and Noriko never tires of watching her paint, the soft explosions of water colour given shape and meaning by her mother's skillful hand, teasing whole worlds from nothing but the tip of a wet brush.

When the world was alive, her mother had illustrated children's books. Her series of books about an orphan panda, traveling the world and getting in all manner of trouble and misfortune were famous and sold everywhere. Noriko's mother had helped tell stories in languages she could not even speak. This is another way in which storytellers are magic. Noriko had been proud of her mother, though at the same time she had been slightly jealous of the other children, all of whom could believe in that panda, never having seen it spring to false life on the cluttered surface of her mother's desk. Noriko had seen behind the curtain, she knew how the trick was done, Noriko could never pretend the panda was anything but water and pigment. When her friends had gathered around well-worn copies they had seen only magic and adventure, Noriko had seen hard work, late nights and arguments with the writer. Somewhere, deep inside, Noriko had resented having that magic taken away from her.

But now, much older, and forced to live in a world of *apparent* magic, a world of robot Samurai, of monsters in the sea and sky, of ghosts in the air, she wished she could pull back the curtain and see the real world behind it all once more. She wished that more than anything because the alternative was her greatest fear. She feared there *was* no curtain, she feared the magic was now *real*.

Perhaps, if she could only get home again, if she could only see her parents in the flesh rather than in the storybook of her own memories, she would be able to find the real world again.

Chapter Three

NORIKO CLIMBS OUT of the amniotic vat, the liquid dripping off her. She wants to be clean.

There is nobody to see her in the automated factory as she wanders around its corridors. We are the only witnesses, the only ones who can picture her, slick and grotesque, leaving a dripping slug trail of the amniotic liquid behind her as she tries to find somewhere to hose herself down, perhaps even a change of clothes. She knows there must be clothes here somewhere, uniforms for the new children of HA/HA. Eventually she finds them, a room stacked with vacuum packed, plain white jumpsuits, not dissimilar to her own, and a row of ceiling mounted showers. She throws her own clothes away and showers herself clean, then puts on a new jumpsuit and makes her way back out into the world of New Tokyo.

*   *   *

PASSING THROUGH THE Ward of Learning, the empty streets suddenly fill with new faces, the children of HA/HA moving between their programming and behavioural sessions. Noriko blends in, keeping her head down, pretending that she too is en route to her lessons, to receive the wisdom of HA/HA. As she passes by the classrooms she hears the pre-programmed curriculum, a gentle, female voice, offering its skewed version of history, of ethics, of the world outside.

'New Tokyo is the heart,' the voice says, 'at the centre of the body of the world. Outside there is chaos, outside there is confusion. You are lucky to live here. You are lucky to have been born to HA/HA. When the rest of the world eventually crumbles away New Tokyo will still stand, New Tokyo is forever, New Tokyo is all.'

The children of HA/HA sit and receive this wisdom with no apparent emotion. They stare at the big screens that show the mask HA/HA wears: that soft, matronly face, those kind, kind eyes. That face looks as if it is the kindest face in the world. Those giant cheeks, a metre high in glistening HD, look as if they would make the softest of beds. A place to lie down and be safe, warmed by the heat of HA/HA.

*   *   *

IN REALITY OF course, HA/HA has no face. HA/HA is information. HA/HA is code. Gods cannot be made of flesh, that would ruin them, they must be like air, they must be impossible to touch or see.

Noriko barely listens to the lessons, just walks along, heading towards the harbour. She has no need of HA/HA's learning, she likes the world the way she believes it to be and has no wish to change her view.

Do you think she's right? Is it a kind of arrogance, or even madness, to refuse to bend in the wind? HA/HA's world is here, HA/HA's world is more than Noriko's beliefs could ever change. What do *you* think the world is like? Do *you* think it's yours? Do *you* think it exists because you believe it? Do *you* shape existence with your will?

Perhaps we all do. We know nothing except that we *think* we know. Knowing is an extension of thought and all thought is subjective. Who is to say what is real anymore?

You are confused. Don't be, picture it like this: you could be dreaming. All of this could be a fantasy that exists only in your own head. You can never know otherwise, not for sure, not *really*. So the best thing is to just believe and let the world stand the way you wish.

Now listen while I tell you more of Noriko's world.

*   *   *

AT THE HARBOUR, the sun is turning the sea into a bright white sheet of light. People are beginning to gather. Some of them are the new children of HA/HA (one day they will be the only ones left alive here, an entire city of perfect, conforming children) some are the people who lived here before, the people who remember the world before The Change rewrote it. How can you tell? You look at their eyes. The ones who look haunted, the ones who look as if restful sleep is something only experienced in memory—*they* are the old residents, *they* are the ones who know what they have lost.

'What's going on?' Noriko asks, intentionally approaching one of the older residents, the ones who seem real.

The man is in his late fifties, with a nervous tic in his right eye that forces him to keep blinking. He gives Noriko a quick, nervous glance. 'Don't you know?' he asks, 'hasn't your mother told you?'

Noriko thinks about this for a moment and realises that he thinks she is one of the new children of HA/HA, an easy mistake to make given she's dressed like one.

'No,' she replies, 'nobody's told me.'

The man stares at her then, as if confused by what she's said. Noriko can't see why he would be, it was simple enough. 'I really don't know,' she insists.

Eventually he shrugs and then nods towards the sea. 'Kaiju coming,' he says. 'They picked it up on the long range radar and are preparing to fight.'

Noriko has heard of the Kaiju but never seen one. For the first couple of weeks after The Change they had come often, bursting onto land and attacking both buildings and people. Then, once HA/HA had taken full control and instituted her security protocols, instigating hunts offshore to destroy the creatures in their underwater nests, the sightings had become rare.

Noriko knows she shouldn't loiter. Somewhere, the Electric Samurai will still be scouring the air for traces of her life signs. Still, she decides, there's just as much chance of her being found while on the move as there is standing still, why not take the chance and maybe see a miracle?

'Have you seen one before?' she asks the man, who clearly still doesn't trust her, looking at her through narrowed eyes as if that will make her duplicity more clear.

'Of course,' he says, 'who hasn't?'

'Me,' Noriko admits, 'I've heard of them but never seen one.'

'You must be new then,' he replies, looking out across the water where that perfect, glowing surface is beginning to froth and bubble, 'everyone's seen one at some time or another.'

'I'm not what you think,' she tells him, 'I've just never had the opportunity before.'

He shrugs, it's clear he really doesn't care what she's pretending to be.

The water continues to churn, the Kaiju is approaching the surface.

'Where are the Mechs?' Noriko asks. 'Shouldn't they be here by now?'

'They'll come,' the man replies, looking over his shoulder, 'your mother always times these things precisely.'

'She's not my mother,' Noriko tells him. 'I'm on my way home to find my mother, and my father.'

He looks at her again, but this time his face isn't cynical it's just surprised. 'You really are a strange one, aren't you?' he says.

There's no time for her to reply as that's when the surface of the sea finally breaks and the Kaiju rises up into the air. Noriko, for all that she has seen post-Change, is shocked into silence by it. It has a huge, insect-like head, a pair of compound eyes dividing the shoreline up into a grid of avaricious interest. Antennae drip with sea water, glistening like broadcast aerials as they quiver and twitch. Its body is more reptilian, scaled skin pulled into irregular, spiked crests, like the surface of a roughly iced cake. Water cascades between the scales, bringing with it fronds of seaweed, crustaceans and small fish, dropping back into the sea beneath it.

Its arms are the only part of it that look aquatic,

hefty tentacles that coil, suckers puckering and spitting saltwater as they reach for something to grab, tear and snap.

'It looks a bit silly,' says Noriko.

'They always do,' the man admits. 'I once saw one with the head of a cat, all hissing and fangs.'

'It's too many different types of thing, insect, lizard, crustacean. It would be scarier if it picked one type of animal and stuck to it.'

'You can tell it that as it's biting your head off,' he suggests, looking over his shoulder again. 'HA/HA really is cutting it fine today, the Mechs should be here by now.'

It's almost as if this brings them, the sound of their thrusters now cutting through the air. Their contrails are the most visible thing about them, trailing behind the black darts that only become defined when they're almost directly overhead. Their designs are divergent, some broken into pairs: jointed, slender ships, cruising in a v-shape, stocky rectangles, their surface bristling with weaponry; a pair of spider-like vehicles, an oval centre ringed by jointed appendages; a mother craft, muscular and slower-moving. Whipping around them is a sphere ship, its wide windscreen glinting and reflecting back the image of the rearing Kaiju.

'They're smaller than I thought they would be,' Noriko says, 'they don't look like they could stop it.'

'Just you wait and see.'

For a moment it looks as if the ships intend to crash but then, at the point of impact, they slow and shift into formation, one locking into another. The mothership becomes the torso, the V-ships fold out into limbs, the spider-ships, hands. Finally, the sphere docks at the front, swiveling on a gimbal to become the head, staring down at the Kaiju below.

'Now you see,' the man says, and he can't resist a smile, perhaps remembering childhood fantasy as the new, combined weight of the UltraMech drops from the air, multiple retro rockets controlling the movement of its metal limbs as it grabs the Kaiju and begins to wrestle, great plumes of water towering up around them.

The creature screeches in anger, mandible mouth opening up to let loose the sound from its reptilian throat.

Its tentacles wrap and curl around its metal attacker, trying to break it apart, but the magnetic clamps are far too strong and the creature screeches again as the UltraMech electrifies its hull and shocks the creature. The Kaiju falls back, maybe wanting space to regroup, to rethink how to win this battle. Noriko, cocking her head and looking deep into its compound eyes, decides that the Kaiju is not a creature that thinks. It exists to do only one thing: destroy. It is a concept, a monster to scare and smash and break, it is not something that has a life outside those activities. This is not something that sits down calmly to eat, to watch its offspring play, this is not something with a backstory.

Her mother has talked to her about monsters. She has painted many in her time. Her mother always insists that the best monsters have a real life, they have all the things that heroes have: emotions, needs, things that drive them to do what they do. 'Monsters,' her mother once said, 'are just nice people that have been broken.'

That is not something she believes about the Kaiju. The Kaiju is just there to fill the sky and seem impressive.

She finds that interesting. Of course, she is only guessing but deep down she's sure she's right. What sort of world is this now when ciphers walk the streets? When plot devices rear their strange, ugly heads only to have them beaten?

She watches as the UltraMech gives the beast no quarter, pounding at it until the sea turns black and thick. The Kaiju gives one last scream then slides down into the foam of seawater and its own flesh, a huge column of water rising up in its wake and raining down on the harbour, bringing chunks of the Kaiju with it.

The onlookers gather around these pieces of monster. Some fascinated, some just wanting to poke at them or kick them as if they too are playing their part in the creature's destruction. The old man Noriko has been talking to walks over to one, purple and sinewy, quivering as air escapes from it with a wet, blubbery fart. He spits on it, then walks away back to whatever he calls a life.

Noriko thinks about going to look but decides that now it's reduced to pieces the creature is even less real, even less worthy of attention.

She looks up in the sky as the UltraMech separates back out into its constituent parts. The crowd cheers as they fly away, some of them shouting out the names of the pilots they know to be flying them. Noriko wonders. Noriko wonders if the Mechs are any more real than the Kaiju.

THEN NORIKO LOOKS directly at you. Yes! You! The ones who are hearing her story.

And, just for a moment, she wonders if she is real too.

Chapter Four

HELLO? ARE YOU still there?

I thought I lost you for a moment. It went dark and I couldn't feel you out there, couldn't sense your attention. Maybe I already lost it, maybe you don't really want to hear my story. *Noriko's* story. Maybe.

Maybe you want to hear about something else? Something prettier perhaps? There are other stories, it's true, of *course* there are. But I don't know them. I only know this one. Noriko's story is the only story I have to tell. That is my flaw I suppose, my blindness, my limitation. But then, I am nothing special, in fact I was nothing at all, not really, not until I met Noriko and all of a sudden my mind opened and I understood things that had previously been just blank spaces to me.

Sometimes I wonder if that might have been better. To

have remained blank. To have remained dull. To have been nothing.

But there's no point in thinking those thoughts. What is done is done. I am this now, I am a storyteller and while you may wish I had more than one story to tell, I do not. So I will speak and you will listen, because otherwise there's no point to any of this.

NORIKO HANGS BACK as the Mechs fly back to wherever it is they live (imagination or reality, she really isn't sure). She watches the crowd start to thin out, to rejoin whatever lives they possess. Then she notices someone and, for the first time in what feels like a lifetime, she thinks she has seen a person with real purpose.

It's an old woman, wrapped in mismatched shawls and blankets. As the slight wind ruffles them, Noriko realizes some of them aren't even that. The old woman is wearing whatever she could find. A piece of a child's towel, illustrated with a cartoon character, a superhero, all muscles and teeth, its confident face obscured by dirt; a piece of bedlinen; a plastic sheet; a ragged section of awning, torn from a shop-front. This is truly a woman who has fallen off the conventional pathways of life.

In some parts of the world, since The Change brought us low, the old woman would not have looked so out of place. Noriko has heard people say that there are some cities that have gone completely wild, places where no normal being could even dream of living. Here in New Tokyo, under the controlling influence of HA/HA, the caring heel of mother, normality—or at least the vague appearance of it—is still aspired to. Mother likes her children to have order. That is why many parts of the prefecture are now forbidden, cordoned off. Not only to keep the citizens out but to keep the madness, the *real* madness, in.

This old woman looks like she belongs to one of those parts of the city. This old woman looks like she belongs on the fringe.

As Noriko watches, the old woman gathers up several pieces of the Kaiju and drops them, dripping wet, into a golf caddy. She wheels the caddy away from the harbour and Noriko decides to follow.

The old lady has some sort of illness. Noriko can no longer judge if it is a disease of the body or the mind. As she moves, she twitches and shouts, convulsing, yelping, dancing along the road. She looks to Noriko like a woman who is being pestered by a swarm of bees.

You think that such behaviour would draw attention? That just shows what you know about people. People do not like strange, even now, in a world that is nothing but. They turn away from it, close their eyes to it, they pretend that it is not there. So, when this woman walks down the street nobody looks at her. When she yelps at some unseen poke from an invisible finger, nobody turns to see what's wrong. She becomes invisible, one more symptom of the madness that nobody really wants to admit to.

Only Noriko watches. Only Noriko cares.

The old woman skirts the edge of Shinjuku Gyoen. Do you remember the Imperial Gardens before they became one of HA/HA's forbidden zones? Maybe you walked there once? Maybe you remember the cherry blossom? Now, of course, the trees have teeth and the chrysanthemums whisper truths that nobody can bear to hear. But back then, before The Change, it was a place of beauty. People still look towards it and remember, sometimes they cry at what they lost.

The old lady doesn't even glance, she has no time for flowers. She just keeps twitching and yelling, hopping and skipping, moving on towards Sendagaya.

Noriko does too.

Every now and then, the old lady stops and collects more things for her caddy. She hunts in the waste bins, pulling out cardboard and paper. She snaps off low branches from trees. At one point she even steals a wooden chair from outside an abandoned street café, dragging it behind her, its legs clattering on the road with every bump and twitch.

It is getting dark by the time the old lady stops and Noriko is confused at how much time has passed. Has the day gone so quickly? There is little point in doubting it as the light fades and the buildings begin to light up all over the prefecture. Night in New Tokyo is a very different world and normally Noriko is careful to spend it somewhere she knows well.

Soon it will be time for HA/HA's curfew. This is a new rule under her regime, put in place, so HA/HA has claimed in her announcements on the video screens, in order to keep her children safe. At night things roam. At night things hunt. So HA/HA wants all her precious babies tucked up in their homes where nothing can happen to them that isn't part of HA/HA's plan.

It's too late for Noriko to worry about it now, she has spent too long being distracted by this strange old woman, and now she has no choice but to see the thing through.

The old woman has come to rest near the train station. As Noriko watches her unpack her golf caddy, she can hear the sounds of the ghost trains as they scream up and down the tracks. Noriko has watched those trains from a distance, their bodies like bone cages, filled with the blank-faced dead as they are ferried towards whatever afterlife awaits the dead post-Change.

The old woman notices Noriko; perhaps she always had.

'You may as well come and sit with me,' she shouts, after she has deposited the pieces of Kaiju meat on the ground and then dug deeper in her caddy for a blanket, kindling and matches. 'Stand over there or sit over here, it makes no odds to me, but you'd be more comfortable and I'd have some company.'

The old woman builds a small fire, breaking down the chair, bundling up the paper waste and setting light to it with one of her matches. By the time Noriko has decided to join her, the flames are catching and it crackles and pops on the pavement, lighting up the old woman's face and turning it into a hollowed out bag of features, all thrown in together with shadows.

'Oh,' the old woman says as Noriko draws close, 'I didn't know you were one of her lot.'

'Who?' asks Noriko.

'HA/HA,' the old woman says, spitting into the fire with a glutinous hiss, 'I can tell from your clothes.'

'I stole them,' Noriko explains, 'I'm not what you think.'

'Who is these days?' the old woman admits, pulling out a knife from her caddy. By the time it's even occurred to Noriko that the old woman might mean her harm, the knife is slicing through a piece of the Kaiju.

'You're not going to eat that?' Noriko asks, as the old woman takes a paper-thin slice of black and purple flesh and folds it between her fingers.

'Got to eat,' the old woman replies, poking the oily parcel between thin, chapped lips, 'and it's not as bad as you'd think. In fact it's one of the few pleasures left in this hollow place.'

The old woman chews and, even though it's been sliced thin, Noriko can hear the sinew pop and crunch between weak teeth.

'If you eat enough of it,' the old woman continues, 'it gives you dreams. You sure you don't want some? I've plenty to spare.'

'I'm not hungry,' says Noriko.

The old woman shrugs, swallows and begins cutting another slice.

'So what are you, if you're not what I think?' she asks as she begins to curl the next slice into a tube.

'My name's Noriko, I'm going home.'

'Good luck with that,' says the old woman, the words coming with a whistle as she breathes through the tube of Kaiju flesh. 'I don't think anyone's home is still there anymore, not really.'

'I think mine will be,' says Noriko, 'and my mother and father, they wouldn't go anywhere without me.'

'Maybe they didn't have a choice. You think of that?'

The old woman is digging right at the bottom of her golf caddy and pulls out a bottle of soft drink. It's a cheery looking bottle, all suns and primary colours. When she opens it, it hisses.

'It seems to me,' the old woman continues, taking a big mouthful of the drink and belching her appreciation, 'that choice is something we left behind with everything else.'

'I know they're there,' Noriko explains, 'I don't know how, but I do.'

The old woman shrugs again and offers Noriko the bottle. Noriko means to refuse it but somehow doesn't dare, worried that it would be seen as rude to refuse both the food and the drink. She takes a small sip and is surprised by the taste of it, she can't remember the last time she tasted something so sweet.

'Thank you,' she says, passing the bottle back. 'It's very nice.'

'It makes me pee all night long,' says the old woman, 'but even that seems like fun these days.'

She begins to slice another piece of meat. 'One last piece,' she says, 'any more and my dreams will be nightmares.'

'Does it really give you dreams?' Noriko asks.

'Oh yes,' says the old woman, 'dreams that make your brain boil.'

'What do you dream?'

'Oh,' replies the old woman, 'I dream all sorts of things. About friends that are gone, husbands I've outlived, worlds vanished. What do you dream?'

'I don't really remember,' Noriko admits, 'just flashes, but I think they're dreams from when I'm little. Our house, mainly, walking through it, watching.'

'As you get older you'll find more things to dream about, more things to scare you when your eyes are closed and the night falls.'

The old woman twitches again, her leg shooting out straight as if tugged by an invisible string.

'Why do you do that?' Noriko asks, before she's even wondered if it's a rude question.

'My body's not always my own, dear. It shakes about all over the place. I've got used to it.'

'But, if your body's not yours who else's is it?'

The old woman smiled. 'These days? I suppose you'd say it was HA/HA's.'

Chapter Five

WHEN THE OLD woman goes to sleep, Noriko sits and looks out on the city at night. She likes to do this because night is the only time New Tokyo can really be beautiful. Darkness hides horrors, sometimes we even want it to.

She watches the lights in the apartment buildings, taking it in turns to switch on and off, like a logic diagram. Overhead, drones buzz like fat luminescent dragonflies, ferrying supplies back and forth as the factories come into their own, working through the night to process and burn and mince and grind. Noriko has heard it said that the food plants are using corpses now, old meat pulped to feed the new. New Tokyo is a bubble, it has no wish to import anything from outside itself, the city must be self-sufficient.

After a couple of hours, the cloudfish bloom, brightly coloured jellyfish that throw their luminescence against the underside of the clouds as they hover and bounce. Sometimes their tentacles brush against the tops of buildings releasing a small shower of sparks, blue rain that fizzes and sputters as it falls towards the cold earth.

Noriko doesn't know where the cloudfish come from. She thinks they are part of the same magic as the Kaiju. The Change was like a virus of potential, in its wake anything can happen, even jellyfish in the sky. What do they eat? Where do they go when they're not floating above the city? She is just starting to wonder if these questions are even possible to answer. She is beginning to think that sometimes, now, things just *are*.

At one point, a cloudfish floats close to the street she's sitting in. It's elongated and glowing violet. Its skirts waft with a fluid quality that sets a breeze amongst the branches of the taller trees. When it passes over her she can feel that slight breeze, city air displaced onto her face by a miracle.

A group of men from an apartment block to her left have designs on catching it. Perhaps they've also heard the stories of what's in the processed food these days.

They've rigged up a small promontory on the corner of the building, a triangle of ladders and rope that allows them to reach out with hooks made from coathangers and broomhandles. Shouting directions to one another, they wave their weapons at the cloudfish, hoping to tear into its soft flesh with the hooks and drag it onto the roof where they can fillet it. Noriko wonders what such thin, semi-transparent flesh will taste like. Would it fizz on the tongue or just melt?

One of the men pierces it but he is now in a dangerous position. Either his friends will be able to hold him down or he'll be dragged skyward by the cloudfish. Perhaps his hunger has blinded him to the danger because this is what happens. One of the other men makes a grab for his ankle but can't get a grip so off he goes, floating up, hanging from the broomhandle, screaming as he realizes there is now nothing below him but certain death. His hands begin to slip on the pole and Noriko thinks she should probably look away as only one thing can happen next.

She is wrong. He doesn't fall. When the cloudfish's skirt touches him, he is transfixed, a glowing flesh cross, his bones visible through glowing skin and muscle. He remains that way, hair upright, mouth twisted in a comical smile as the cloudfish continues its journey over the city.

The rest of the fishermen watch him go, shoulders low, then throw down their hooks and head back to their apartments. No doubt they'll try again tomorrow night.

Noriko turns her attention to a different pair of cloudfish, turned on their sides so they appear like pulsating moons. They hover some miles away, way up in the sky, and appear to dance with one another, spiraling, bouncing, changing places and then, finally, merging. For a few seconds they are one, bright, beautiful celestial body then they part again. Their dance is over and they go their separate ways.

The cloudfish only swarm for about an hour, after that the sky is once again clear and Noriko goes back to watching the lights. After the magic of the cloudfish, they seem too sterile, too formulaic now and she wonders about sleep.

The old woman starts screaming.

At first Noriko wonders if it's the dreams the old woman predicted, didn't she say that too much of the meat would bring nightmares? Then she sees something that confuses her. Just for a moment is seems that the woman is not alone, a portion of shadow surrounds her, moving with her as she sits upright and then jumps to her feet.

Confused, Noriko runs, jumping behind one of the matter refuse tanks that have been placed outside the larger apartment buildings (HA/HA insists her children recycle). She watches as the old woman steps out into the street, her arms and legs moving stiffly. She looks like a child's action figure, badly jointed and unable to appear truly human. For a moment Noriko questions the shadow she saw earlier, there's nothing there now as the old woman spins out onto the street and begins to move along it. Then, again, Noriko catches a flicker of movement, a darkness that isn't the old woman's shadow yet clings to her as if it must be. As soon as she notices it, like before, it's gone.

She follows.

The old woman is shouting curses and threats, as if she's being dragged against her will. Is there something there then? Something controlling her? Then Noriko wonders if this is what the old woman meant earlier when she said her body was not her own. Is it now being used by the other person? If so, what do they want with it? Where are they hoping to go?

Keeping out of sight, she follows the old woman as she jerks awkwardly along the street, eventually coming to a junction and turning right. She hops and shouts down the middle of the road, the curfew keeps all but the automated drones away so there's nothing to collide with her as she dances between traffic lanes, passing under a large illuminated sign offering a flickering prayer to the electronic mother.

'Mother knows best,' the sign says, as the face of a young girl smiles and looks up into the beneficent glow of what could be a sun or the smiling, hungry teeth of HA/HA herself.

A flicker of movement in the street ahead tears Noriko's attention away from the sign as another jerking, twitching figure emerges from an alleyway and marches alongside the old woman.

This new figure is that of a young man. His clothes are as tatty as the old woman's, random and mismatched but he doesn't shout as she does. In fact, he appears to be asleep, his head nodding against his chest as his arms reach up, strangely limp at the wrists. Everything about him is loose and now Noriko can see both of them another image comes to mind: that of the Ningyōtsukai, the puppeteers in the theatre, controlling their large dolls by hiding behind them, dressed head to toe in black; theatrical gods, making their creations dance to whatever narrative the play demands.

With this thought, she once again thinks she sees something hovering around the old woman and the new man who has joined her. A flash, that is all. A sense that there are four people moving down the street, not two.

And now more: a small child, a middle-aged man, a beautiful woman... all of them wear clothing that suggests they are living rough, like the old woman. These are the disenfranchised, the people living outside HA/HA's program. Noriko wonders if she might be next. For a second, she considers running away, to put some space between herself and whatever this is that is happening. Noriko doesn't want to share their fate, Noriko just wants to go home. What business is this of hers?

But the thought doesn't linger. This is because Noriko is better than you. Noriko is better than me. Noriko is brave.

She follows. Soon there are thirty people walking along in front of her. They are all different ages and genders, the only thing they share is the fact that they are outsiders. Noriko is surprised there are so many. HA/HA likes to pretend that most of the citizens of New Tokyo, most of her happy little children, are part of her design. They live in their apartments, they work in their menial jobs, they do as they are told and they like it. To see all these people in front of her, all people who have turned their back on HA/HA and are living on the periphery, makes Noriko wonder how powerful HA/HA really is.

Ahead of them stand the twin chimneystacks of one of the processing plants. It looks like a goat's head made of glass and steel and brick, great plumes of black smoke curling from its horns. Its mouth is wide open, a neon strip-lit warehouse, visible beyond sliding-door teeth of corrugated steel. Forklift trucks and drones dip in and out of the warehouse, empty on the way in and fully-laden on the way out, taking their heavy pallet-loads to where they need to be.

The procession of people is marched past this and around the side of the factory to a ramp that leads them into the main body of the building. Noriko is concerned that once inside, with the bright strip-lighting, she'll no longer be able to hide. Should she give up on going any further? Then she sees that the factory floor is filled with so many vats, so much equipment, that she can easily slip around unnoticed. She's used to being careful; there's a reason the Electric Samurai, for all their effort, have never managed to catch her.

The extra lighting does help reveal one thing though: the bodies of the puppeteers. It's still no more than the odd, momentary glimpse, but away from the night, away from the darkness, it's hard for even these things to hide. Their limbs are long, their fingers extending and curling around their puppets in a way that makes Noriko think of the tentacles hanging from the cloudfish. Fingers simply shouldn't have that many joints in them.

The puppeteers are always moving, always dancing around their charges, constantly tugging, pushing, nudging to keep them on track. If only they would stand still, just for a single second, Noriko is sure she could get a proper look at one of them. Maybe she doesn't want to.

The procession splits up, each puppeteer leading their dancing human towards a different vat. It occurs to Noriko only now that she's about to see something she really, really doesn't want to see.

She follows the old woman, hoping that there may be an opportunity for her to help. The old woman is strange, she is possibly ill, but she showed her kindness and that means Noriko can't just stand by and let something awful happen to her. Not if she can help it.

The old woman is led to a wheeled set of steps that are

parked next to one of the vats. Step after clanking step, she is led up to the lip of the vat. Noriko is at a loss as to what she should do. It's so bright! There are so many of them! If she runs out and tries to fight the puppeteer what possible chance does she have? She is small and it is not. She is alone and it is not. All that will happen is that she will join the old woman in the vat that she is now teetering over.

And then, the old woman, who has long since given up on shouting at the creature that has dragged his this far, looks up and sees Noriko, hiding behind a deactivated cleaning drone.

'Don't worry,' the old woman says, 'this is just something new for you to dream about.'

All across the factory, screens begin to descend from the roof. Happy music is played from hidden speakers, echoing and distorting thanks to the terrible acoustics of this steel barn.

'Don't worry,' says the voice of HA/HA as the screens show pictures of smiling children, skipping in a dream of a garden. It's a place that Noriko is quite sure exists only in the pretty fiction of pixels. 'What happens to you now is for the good of all. We have a big society. And in a big society everyone needs to play their part. Those who refuse to do so, who insist on trying to stay off-grid, must be encouraged from their views. They must, if need be, be forced to offer what they can. They must contribute. You do so now, and Mother thanks you.'

Looking around the factory, Noriko can see all of the people she's followed being pushed into their vats. Some scream, others drop silently, perhaps they are asleep, perhaps they have fainted. The bodies hit the bottom of the vats with a resounding clang, repeated throughout so that it's like a steel drum band playing off-key. Then the motors begin to grind. Cogs turn. Blades whir. The screaming is very brief.

Hiding her eyes behind her fingers, Noriko now knows that the rumours about the food are not the entire truth. HA/HA is not simply making use of the dead, she is making use of anyone or anything that does not match her criteria as a worthwhile citizen. HA/HA does not like waste.

Noriko cannot bear to stay and listen to the pulp as it is pumped into the pipes. She doesn't want to think of the old woman, whose drink and company she shared, now turned to nothing but a pale pink sludge.

She turns to run but she finds herself surrounded by Ningyōtsukai. She can see them now. They allow it. Their dark fluid limbs moving like willow trees in the wind. One of them reaches up to its head and pulls away the black mask it wears to show her a smile made of soft, gelatinous teeth.

Noriko pushes her way past them, running through the

factory and out of the door she came in. She can hear the puppeteers behind her, even though their feet are as soft as the rest of them, no more than brushing the ground as they run with boneless strides.

She doesn't think she can outrun them but then she sees a way: a drone, loaded-up with a pallet of the special, flavoursome paste this factory produces, taking off and aiming for the one place she wants to be: *somewhere else*. She grabs hold of the drone and lets it take her. It lifts her up, the curling fingers of the puppeteers slapping against her heels as she soars high above them, over the fence, into the darkness. Away.

Chapter Six

IMAGINE! THAT'S HOW stories work, remember, I tell you things and then you imagine they're happening to you. So it's not just Noriko hanging off the drone, rising up above the city, it's you too. You remember the man that found himself lifted up by the cloudfish? Remember that moment he must have felt when, looking down, he realized that letting go was no longer an option? That's going through Noriko's mind right now.

(Yes, yes... I know, this is still the past, though we are getting closer to the present, if it's still bothering you to hold two times as current, as *now*, in your mind.)

The higher up she goes, the more the wind catches her and her grip on the drone isn't perfect. She just grabbed it of course, a spontaneous decision, with no concern as to longevity, this is not something she *planned*.

Earlier she had looked up at this sky, considering it

as you would a foreign world, a place where cloudfish dance, where freedom seems possible, cut loose from the restrictions of the earth, of the city. But the ground still pulls at her, this *is* a foreign world, as foreign as the depths of the ocean or the airless absence of space. This is not somewhere she was designed to live. She can't fly. She can't even float. With every moment gravity is pulling, the ground wants her back, and if she gives in, it will rush to meet her with a sudden, bone-crunching kiss.

She does her best to steady herself, pulling herself up so that she's resting on the drone. But even that's a problem because HA/HA is not about wastage, the drone is carrying the weight it's designed to carry. If it could really take the extra load Noriko represents it would be carrying it in the form of another pallet. So it dips and groans, its engine whining as it tries to carry out its programmed task despite this new, uncomfortable set of variables.

And it tries, because machines do, machines are not built to give up, they just keep trying until they can't manage anymore. Noriko knows this and she can only hope that the drone will be stronger than its designers give it credit for. And maybe it would have succeeded, despite its erratic flight, despite the smell of burning from within its motor. But then... then it experiences another unforeseen variable.

Noriko doesn't know what the noise is when she first hears it. A loud, percussive sound, from the far side of the drone. She thinks it's probably part of the drone's mechanism snapping under the strain. When it happens again she understands it for what it is because she can see the hole the bullet leaves behind. Someone is shooting at the drone.

She thinks of the hunters, desperate to catch a cloudfish to bolster up their larders and she realizes the drone makes an even more obvious target. Someone wants to bring it down so they can steal its cargo. Maybe, she thinks, they'll consider her a bonus, something fresh to roast in their ovens or fry on their electric hobs.

This is all too much for the drone and it veers, so suddenly and violently it's all but a miracle that she doesn't lose her grip right then and there. She manages to hang on with one hand as it heads towards the ground. It doesn't just drop. Like I say, it's a machine and it doesn't give up easily. With a terrible scream of its motor it fights to stay airborne, getting lower and lower in jerky, hopeless spurts. There is another shot but this one goes wide, possibly whoever is firing can see that this is one hunt that's failed. They've brought the drone down but at such an angle it will be too far away to track and collect. Not that anyone would dare to retrieve it from the place it's falling towards. Even Noriko, most of her concentration taken up by simply holding on, is aware of the high wall they fly over, her heels brushing the top of it as they pass. They're entering one of the forbidden zones. They're entering the Ward of the Fire Ghosts.

I'VE MENTIONED THE forbidden zones. The Imperial Gardens of course, with its hostile flowers. Then there's the Ward of Dreaming where nobody can set foot and stay awake, sent straight into a sleep that lasts as long as your body takes to wither and die (possibly longer, who can say, who can ever *really* say?). There's also the Ward of Downside Up, where gravity is in constant confusion. If you manage to survive suddenly falling against the buildings to either side of you, you certainly won't survive falling upwards, beyond the clouds.

The Ward of the Fire Ghosts is, perhaps, not quite as immediately lethal. It is a place of old memories, a place of the past. Certainly that will be one reason HA/HA hates it. HA/HA does not believe in yesterday, HA/HA only believes in tomorrow. This is not to say that the Ward of Fire Ghosts is, in any way safe, of course it isn't. I do not think there is anywhere in New Tokyo that can claim that. But Noriko does at least stand a chance, if she can be careful, if she can avoid the ghosts.

What's that? You don't believe in ghosts? Then you are a fool. Aside from the fact that this story should have made it clear that anything can happen in the prefecture now, *anything at all*, ghosts are not new. Ghosts have always been real. Maybe not in the way that you are imagining, as thinking spirits that inhabit the world, still driven by desires and plans, but as history with weight. Sometimes, the things that happen in the world are too terrible not to leave scars. These scars never fade. These scars are ghosts. And the bombs that fell, so many years ago now, created many, many ghosts.

I do not intend to debate the politics of those bombs. It is not part of my story and… and, yes, if I am truthful with you, it is a debate that is beyond my limited skills. I am new at this, this is my first real story (I know, my *only* story) and while I will admit that, as I repeat it, I am finding the telling of it easier, the words more readily coming to mind, a discussion on the ethics of warfare is not something I can consider. It is too complex. It is a history in which everyone is wrong. I will just explain the basics. There was a war and Japan was part of that war. As in all wars, it did things of which it cannot be proud. The reprisal for these actions, and an attempt to ensure no such actions occurred again, was an extended bombing campaign. If Japan surrendered, the bombing would stop. Japan would not surrender. Even knowing it could not win, that all that could happen is that more of its people would die, Japan would not surrender. Between November 1944 and the 15th of August 1945, the skies brought death. Planes dropped their firebombs on us and we *burned*. Hundreds of thousands died, many, many more lost their homes. Perhaps this is also why Tokyo has reacted to The Change the way it has, perhaps this is why it endures, however strangely, after the events of that catastrophic morning. Because we have done all this before. We have faced the fire and carried on. Eventually, perhaps, we even managed to forget, or at least pretend to have done so.

But not in the Ward of the Fire Ghosts. There the bombs still fall, there the world still burns. And there, battered but not broken (no, never broken) Noriko finds herself waking up, having finally fallen from the drone when it was, thankfully, only a few feet from the ground.

Chapter Seven

SHE SITS UP and sees the wreckage of the drone a few feet away. It has imbedded itself nose-first in a ground of ash and rubble, its spilled contents scattered around it as she could have been, had she not let go when she had.

She has not been here before, is confused by the sight of the crumbling, broken buildings around her. This is not a Tokyo she understands. She is used to a Tokyo that pretends towards normality. A Tokyo that sweeps its dirt and destruction away (even as it sweeps its unwanted citizens away, removed in the darkness never to be seen again, at least until the next time you open a can of food).

She gets to her feet, somewhat unsteadily to begin with as she moves stiff limbs across the uneven rubble, and looks around, trying to get her bearings. She wonders what can have happened here to cause such destruction. Did the people that live here anger HA/HA? Did the beneficent mother strike out at them in order to offer a lesson in obedience? Surely not. If that had been the case then would she not have heard about it? A lesson is hardly instructive if it's not known. Perhaps one of the Kaiju caused the damage? Rearing up out of the water and grinding these buildings beneath an impossible, absurd, scaly foot?

She continues to explore. Trying to find answers in the ruins of a Tokyo that is lost not only in destruction and fire but also time.

She emerges into a wide street, either side littered with the shells of homes. Some appear almost intact (until closer examination reveals their hollow insides, their collapsed floors, their half-standing staircases) some are no more than piles of charred bricks.

The air smells of soot. A vague fog of dust and smoke still hanging around her like fallen clouds.

In one of the destroyed buildings she sees a family sat around a dining table, an impossible tableau of normality, made grotesque by the black, charred state of their bodies. They appear both crisp and yet also sticky. Noriko stares at them for a few minutes. They look like they are about to eat. Two large figures, one at either side of the table, and, in the middle, a smaller body, a child, its tiny, cracked fists resting on the surface of the table. It is a mother and father, she thinks, like mine. And now they are always at home, always together.

Then, one of the larger figures (the mother, she thinks, though the fire has removed any real indication of gender) turns to look at her. Noriko hears the crunching, grinding sound of the neck as it turns, burned flesh cracking as it moves. The figure opens its mouth to show surprisingly white teeth within, and a swollen tongue that has puffed up like a coal, far too big to allow such a mouth to swallow.

Does it mean to speak? To tell Noriko to leave them in peace? To stop staring into their private world, an unwelcome intruder? Noriko doesn't wait to find out, she runs down the street, uncertain as to whether the figure will care enough to rise on blackened legs and follow.

Noriko wonders how best to leave this broken place. In the fall she has lost her sense of direction and can't see beyond the shattered buildings to get her bearings. She decides she needs to gain higher ground. Perhaps, if she can find somewhere to climb up and look out she will see something she recognizes from the rest of the city, something to guide herself by.

At the end of the street (not turning around as she doesn't want to know if the burned mother has followed her, split feet revealing the cooked meat of her soles as she takes step after slow step) Noriko looks to either side and, seeing a semi-intact apartment building to her left, runs towards it.

From the front it could almost appear untouched, but as she circles it, it reveals its insides, like a doll's house opened on its hinges, a zig-zagging staircase to either side and box after box of battered apartments. Scrabbling up a toppled section of wall, she manages to step into one of the exposed stairwells and begins to climb. In places, the steps have been knocked away but enough of their structure remains for her to be able to climb relatively easily for the first few floors. On the fifth floor, such a large hole has been knocked into the concrete that she's forced to risk the remains of the metal handrail that hangs, creaking and bobbing to one side. It squeals with her weight as she pulls herself up but she manages to avoid the gap and leap back onto the steps.

Looking down into the empty shells of the apartments she finds her attention drawn to a painting on one of the walls. It's of a man she does not know, old, regal-looking, painted in such a way as to have his importance, his *majesty*, come through with every stroke. The bottom corner of the painting is burned but somehow the rest has survived. She wonders if it's the Emperor. An old Emperor, one who ruled over a world that made more sense than this one. Thinking of the destruction all around, she wonders if the world has ever made sense.

Finally she reaches the top floor. Her view is blocked by the remains of the stairwell but if she moves into one of the apartments she should be able to look out through the space where the wall would once have been.

At first she thinks she's going to be frustrated by something as simple as a door. With all of the damage, great holes in everything, the door to the closest apartment is stubbornly jammed. This seems a joke in poor taste. She kicks and kicks at the wood and finally it shows signs of moving. Stepping back, she decides that if she runs at it, with all her strength, she can probably knock it open.

Resting flat against the opposite wall, she tenses and then flings herself at the door. With a bang it opens, Noriko falling through it, but behind her there's the sound of falling masonry and she realizes that the door was keeping part of the wall up. She pulls herself along the floor on her hands and knees as bricks and rubble shower down, eventually cowering behind an upturned table as the falling masonry subsides. Looking back towards the doorway, she realizes she's going to have a hard time leaving the way she came in. The wall has tipped in on itself and while she may be able to climb over it she thinks it's more likely the wall will topple onto her.

She thinks in much the same way as the drone did earlier. She will not give up. She will not stop. She will carry on and, when it comes to it, she will figure out a way.

She looks out beyond the apartment and can see the wall she flew over and, beyond it, the Tokyo she knows. Carefully taking hold of what remains of the wall she looks in the other direction and realizes, even more importantly, that this area bridges several sections of New Tokyo. If she cuts through it, heading south, she'll be close to home. This good news makes her care even less about her current predicament. It is all perfection. It is as things should be.

If she can figure out a way of climbing down.

THERE IS ONLY one way that occurs to her. She must lower herself from this apartment to the one below. If she can do that she will be able to get back to the stairway and from there to the ground.

She looks around, hoping to find a hole in the floor that will lead her, relatively easily, to the apartment underneath. Of course there isn't one, because, while Noriko does not believe in gods (especially those like HA/HA who have been born only recently) she is certainly a believer in bad luck and the easy ability with which it punishes those who have the audacity to hope.

So, the only way is to lower herself over the outside edge of the building and swing back inside. This is not an idea she finds pleasing, not least because the sharp edges of the shattered floor look all too likely to break under her weight.

She searches the apartment for something she might be able to use to support herself. Eventually she finds a child's skipping rope and a pair of singed curtains. She rolls the curtains up and ties them together, attaching the skipping rope to the end. It is far from ideal but it will do. It does not need to hold for any length of time, just long enough for her to swing down a few feet.

She spends a little time finding something she can tie the other end of her makeshift rope to. She decides that while the pile of rubble in front of the doorway may be too precarious to climb, it is certainly weighty enough to support her for the brief time she needs it to. The collapsing masonry has pushed the wooden doorframe out of the wall and a corner of it is jutting into the room. Tying the end of the sheet to this, she wraps the end of the skipping rope around one arm and shuffles towards the place where the floor ends in shattered brick and splintered wood. As she gets closer to the edge, she can feel the brickwork beginning to give under her weight so she grabs the rope with her spare hand so that when the bricks finally do fall, as they do now, showering towards the ground, she's got a solid grip as she drops with them. The rope catches on the edge of the floor and she flips backwards into the apartment below. She tries to let go before momentum carries her back towards open air again, but she has wrapped the rope too tightly around her arm and she's forced to try and grab it once more as her feet kick back out into thin air. Above her, she hears the sound of tearing nylon and she knows her rough rope is no longer going to hold. Thankfully, her swing hits its apex and then takes her back into the safety of the lower apartment before the sheet tears completely and she is flung against the far wall.

Sitting up, unwrapping the skipping rope from her arm, she looks towards the doorway, hoping to see free access towards the stairwell. What she sees is a blackened figure sat in a small wooden chair. For a moment she is startled, thinking the burned mother she saw earlier has followed her up here. Then, she realizes that this is a different body. It looks strangely staged, sat upright in its chair, legs at perfect right angles, feet flat on the floor. Its arms are neat by its side, hands folded in its lap. The only thing about the body that is any way untidy is one remarkable plume of hair that juts from the right-hand side of its scalp, sticky and matted with burned skin. Noriko stares at it, remembering the perfect way the other bodies had been sat at their dining table, who would die in such a calm manner? Then she remembers that at least one of the previous bodies was not as dead as it should have been, did it not turn to look at her?

Afraid that this one may do the same, she looks beyond

it towards the doorway (open thankfully) and makes to run through it. She will go past this burned figure and it will not move, it will just sit there as she runs through the doorway and down the stairs.

It grabs her arm as she passes and its sticky hand, that surely should not still be hot, hisses against the fabric of her jumpsuit. She pulls away from it, as much a reaction to the heat as the shock of being grabbed. The figure's arm snaps off at the shoulder, its fingers stuck tight to her forearm. With a cry, she knocks the fingers away, the heat of them having seared the skin beneath her jumpsuit and left bright pink marks to show where they've been.

Noriko runs through the doorway and onto the stairs. Last time she did not dare look to see if she was being followed, this time she daren't not. The figure has tried to stand up but its legs are fixed in a seated position, the muscles and tendons constricted with the heat. Nonetheless it shuffles after her, leaning forward in order to maintain its balance as it makes to follow her down the stairs. She runs and she's descended a floor before she hears it coming after her, hopping with both feet. Thud, thud, thud, two stairs at a time. She looks up and sees it, its remaining arm extended out to help it balance as it jumps. She does not look again, she just runs.

But even as she reaches the fifth floor and the gap in the stairs she cannot ignore the sounds coming from the building all around her. There are many of these burned citizens and now they are awake and coming for her.

She does not even consider using the stair rail to bridge the gap, she just jumps, flying through the air as, in the periphery of her vision, many black shapes begin to converge towards her. She manages to keep upright, colliding with the wall of the stairwell as momentum carries her over the gap and across the last couple of steps before they turn to descend in the opposite direction. It is not only from above that these burned people are appearing and, as she reaches the fourth floor they are already ahead of her, reaching out with arms that creak and opening their chapped mouths (be it to threaten or beg she cannot tell). She keeps her momentum, pushing through them at such speed that even when their hot limbs touch her they don't linger long enough to cause damage. She is aware that again, her movements have left some of them damaged, there is the sound of splitting joints, scattered, brittle fingers and even whole bodies toppling from the stairwell to land with a soft crunch on the ground below. She ignores it all, ignores too the greasy feel of shed skin painted across the white of her jumpsuit as their clutching fingers leave their prints behind.

By the time she reaches the ground, and the toppled piece of wall she climbed up to reach the stairs, these things are in the streets too. Thankfully there is a clear route to the left, the direction she wanted to run anyway, so she slides down the wall and sprints down the street, knowing that if she can only keep ahead of them she may just reach the wall at the edge of this forbidden zone. Once she crosses the wall she knows that she will be safe. She is an intruder here; she is allowed to pass from one part of the city to another, whereas these residents must only exist here in their broken ward.

She turns another slight left, picturing the route she saw from above and hoping that she has remembered it correctly. There will be no time for errors in judgment, she must fly straight and true.

As she runs she becomes aware of a noise in front of her. At first she thinks it must be a drone, maybe sent to retrieve the lost cargo the last one spilled. Then, as it draws closer, grows louder, she realizes that this is something far, far bigger. The engines that drive this flying machine are considerable indeed, this is an all-American construction, brought to life in factories in Washington, Kansas, Georgia and Nebraska. This is a Boeing Baby. This is a B-29 Superfortress, ninety-nine feet long with a wingspan of over one hundred and forty, it passes over Noriko like a dark angel of steel with whirring propellers that dice the air and a belly full of fire and hell.

It cannot be real, she thinks but then neither can the Kaiju, the Mechs, the cloudfish or the creaking, pursuing citizens who want to hold her with hands that sear flame hot.

She cannot run faster, though she tries, as she hears the sound of whistling in the air behind her, the first bombs beginning to fall. She des not turn to see the damage they cause, though she cannot fail but imagine it. Explosions like reality being snapped in half, great plumes of fire and masonry spraying like rain in high wind.

The sound of the engine begins to fade and she wonders if she is to be lucky. Perhaps the flying machine has done its business here today and will not return. Ahead of her, figures are appearing from streets and collapsed buildings. They no longer seem interested in her, just turning their featureless, molten faces towards the sky, watching the plane as it grows smaller into the night. Some stretch their arms upward, as if praising its passing, others extend their hands to one another and where they touch fire blooms, yellow and curling in the meeting of their heat.

Ahead of Noriko now, she can see the wall. It is so high, she has no idea how she will be able to climb it, but she will try, she will certainly try, because behind her she can hear the plane returning. Perhaps this time its bombs will fall on her, perhaps this time history will reach forward through the years that divide them and turn her to ash.

She reaches the wall and is thankful that it is not immune to the fires and explosions that ravage the Ward of the Fire Ghosts. Nowhere is the wall breached but a large section of it is burned and chipped and she can just about force her fingers and toes into holes between the bricks. It is not an easy climb but she eventually makes it to the top, straddling the wall and turning to look back as the bomber drops a second load. Most of the citizens are now holding hands and they look like the paper chains Noriko's mother used to make, a procession of people silhouettes, fire rising from where they touch.

The bombs fall and when they hit the ground the earth reaches for the sky, fire rolling through the static figures in great fists of deep red and smoke grey, punching them to pieces. The air hits Noriko and for a moment she teeters on the top of the wall and then, as her cheeks grow pink with the searing heat, she falls, losing her grip, dropping backwards.

Chapter Eight

OUR STORY IS moving so quickly. Soon it will be done. But will it have worked? Will I have achieved what I hoped to achieve?

If not I will have to start again. And, if need be, *again.* Stories need repetition to grow I think. They need to become well-trodden.

Let us pause for a moment though, to look at Noriko as she hangs there, in the process of falling from the wall that borders the Ward of the Fire Ghosts. Don't worry, she won't hurt herself. I know I shouldn't tell you that, it destroys all of the drama, but really… after all this, you think Noriko will come to harm falling from a slight height? No. That would be ridiculous. This side of the wall is lined with bushes and she will fall into their soft foliage. She will survive this. She has survived many things, it will take more than a wall to stop her.

But just look at her for a moment, while I get my energy back (I am not used to this, talking this long, telling so much). Even after all she's been through, all she's seen, is she not amazing? Is she not the most perfect example of hope you ever saw? Because that's what she is to me, and others like me, who know that the only way we can ever truly be happy is by escaping from the control of HA/HA. Noriko is our only hope.

Oh! Look! I think she is moving! Could this be it? Could this be the moment I hoped for?

'What's happening?' she asks. 'Why am I floating here like this?'

I don't know what to say. I don't have the words to encourage her out of this state and into another. I have been caught in my storyteller's art. My artifice exposed. For a moment I think of talking to her directly but my nerves get the better of me and so... I am a coward, I do the only thing I can, I make the story move again.

NORIKO FALLS INTO the soft foliage of the bushes that line the wall. She is confused, convinced that for a moment her fall was halted, that she had somehow, impossibly, hung in thin air, time frozen around her.

But that cannot have happened, she decides, she must have been dreaming. Perhaps she passed out for a moment as she fell, making her feel like the world just stopped, even if only for a second.

She gets up and looks towards the buildings in front of her. She is close to home now. She is nearly there. She is nearly reunited with her mother and father.

Despite her bruises, despite everything the night has thrown at her, she walks on with speed and hope.

IT'S THE LIGHTS that first attract her to Speaker's Square.

In a way, it's a relief. The hope she had felt has been beginning to wane as she finds that, somehow, she does not remember the way home. *How can I have forgotten?* she asks herself. She knows she's close, that's inarguable, and everything around her is steeped with familiarity and yet her feet are confused, they do not quite know where to go.

She is trying to remember how long it has been since she went home. She is trying to remember what it was that made her leave. These questions hadn't actually occurred to her before and now that fact also makes her scared. What is this hole in her life? What is this big gap—like the hole in the steps she climbed recently, smacked out by some terrible force—why is so much of her life missing?

When she thinks of her mother and father their faces come easily to mind (in fact they never leave it). When she thinks of her home she can picture every room in perfect detail. She can remember what it feels like to lie on her bed. Her feet know the feeling of the wooden floorboards in every room. So why do they not quite remember how to get there?

It is making her scared and angry. So she looks at the lights and she wanders towards them.

The square is huge. In the centre a light fountain spurts beams of neon across plumes of reflective smoke. Lining the square are the Talking Heads, their bronzed, simple features inert until Noriko approaches. Once she's close they all turn to look at her.

'A story?' asks one.

'A good story?' suggest another.

'We know the best stories,' announces a third.

'The only stories that matter,' confirms a fourth.

'I just want to go home,' Noriko sighs, frustrated that not even this square seems familiar to her. 'I'm not in the mood for stories.'

'How can you not be in the mood for stories?' one asks. 'Stories are the only important thing.'

'No they're not,' says Noriko, 'what's real is more important.'

'What's real?' shouts a head from the far end. 'Everything's a story in the end.'

'And everyone,' agrees another.

'That's rubbish,' says Noriko, 'things are real or they're not.'

'But who can ever tell?' the head closest to her asks, 'We believe what we're told and what we're told are stories. Even boring things. Even things about shopping or eating or sleeping, they're all stories once we speak them aloud.'

'And speaking things aloud *makes* them real,' agrees another, 'it's sharing them, taking them from one person and opening them out to everyone else. Nothing is ever really real until it's a story.'

Noriko isn't in the mood to debate this, so she walks away, ignoring the heads that turn to follow her as she passes.

'I don't blame her to be honest,' says one of them to the head on the plinth next to his, 'our stories are all the same anyway. They're all about HA/HA.'

'You can't knock sponsorship,' the head replies.

Noriko is looking up at a street map, trying to make the patterns on it remind her of the things she needs to remember.

'Why do I not recognize you?' she asks.

'I'm not sure we've met,' the map replies.

Noriko is confused for a moment then sees the tiny AI interface in the bottom right-hand corner of the map.

'I didn't know you could speak,' she says, 'sorry.'

'Don't worry,' says the map, 'it surprises most people. I'm supposed to give directions but nobody wants to know them. Nobody walks around in New Tokyo for fun. They leave their homes because they have to, that's all. Everybody knows where they are going.'

'I don't,' Noriko admits.

'Then ask!' The map is genuinely pleased. It has been cursed with a brain capable of considerable things. It is a brain that could happily be installed in the computer of an air traffic control tower or a busy hospital. It is a brain that can reason, learn and multitask. It is a brain the equal to any (excluding, of course, HA/HA) and yet it is relegated to giving directions nobody wants to hear. To make matters worse, it has been given full AI function so not only is it bored but it can really *feel* it.

'I don't know the address,' Noriko admits.

'Oh.' The map is sad. Just for a moment it thought it was going to be able to achieve something.

'Sorry.'

'That's alright, I would have liked to have helped you. I'm really very clever and really very bored. Life is not brilliant in New Tokyo for anyone but it's especially not brilliant for the maps.'

'Don't let HA/HA hear you say that,' Noriko warns it.

'She doesn't listen to people like me,' says the map, 'we're beneath her attention. We're hoi polloi.'

Noriko has not heard the expression before but she can guess at what it means.

'Then maybe you should plan a revolution,' she says, smiling, before walking away.

*   *   *

As SHE LEAVES the square she narrowly misses being caught by a street-cleaning truck as it slowly works its way along. On its back a vast tank of cleaning fluid gurgles and sloshes, working its way through metal pipes to be sprayed from wide nozzles at the front. The liquid hisses as it hits the road surface, dirt vapourising in its lethal spray. Here is another reason for the curfew, Noriko thinks, if you had been sleeping in a doorway as this thing came past, you would have woken up to your face peeling off.

She waits for the truck to pass and crosses over. Looking up at a row of flags that flutter in the air above her, she is suddenly hit by a feeling of familiarity. That sound, the crackling and whipping of silk fabric, opens up a memory for her. This is a sound she knows. It is a sound that is baked into her, deeply. She is going the right way.

Crossing the street she closes her eyes for a moment, listening to the sound and trying to let her feet go wherever they want to. She tries not to get in their way, to not second-guess them.

They move left and she slowly, eyes still closed, lets them take a step at a time, hoping for a memory to kick in.

Have you ever walked with your eyes closed? It starts off easily enough but then, after a few paces, your mind begins to panic, it feels sure that something big is looming, some terrible obstruction that you're going to walk right into and hurt yourself. You try to keep your eyes closed but that imaginary object grows larger and larger in your mind, growing sharper edges and, eventually you have to open your eyes to prove that it isn't there.

At least, that's what people tell me. I wouldn't know, I don't really do much in the way of walking. Maybe it's not true. Certainly it doesn't happen to Noriko. She doesn't even worry about the street cleaning truck that will surely turn around at some point and head back in her direction. She starts to move faster and faster as she lets go with her mind and just lets her feet do what they want. Soon she's running down the street, all of her previous doubts and fears gone as she knows she's on the right track, she knows she's going home.

She turns corners, jumps on and off sidewalks, never once opening her eyes, never once colliding with anything. If she'd stop to think about this for a moment the absurdity of it would certainly rob her of confidence, but she doesn't think, she just runs.

A few minutes later, she stops. Knowing that she has found it. She can smell the familiar smells, hear the distant sounds of the ghost trains on the lines just a few streets away. Even the ground beneath her feet seems to have a shape and texture that she knows.

She is home.

She opens her eyes.

She is not outside the house she has always imagined. She is not looking up into the face of her mother or father. She is outside one of the birthing domes.

Chapter Nine

For a couple of minutes she is simply too confused to move. She stands there, staring at the large, perfect white dome and wonders what has gone so wrong as to lead her here.

She doesn't even notice when the Electric Samurai appear in the sky above, descending to stand on either side of her.

'You are home,' one says, taking her in its huge metal hand and leading her towards the dome.

'This isn't my home,' Noriko whispers, then, quieter, confused, 'is it?'

The Electric Samurai hem her in as she's led into the heart of the dome, into a room identical in design to the one she lost them in only a few hours ago.

A voice speaks to her, pumped from discretely hidden speakers and echoing around the dome.

'Self is glad to see you returned. Self was concerned.'

This, Noriko realizes, is the real voice of HA/HA (and the fact that she is able to realize this rather proves she is not who she thought herself to be. Only HA/HA's children, her *real* children, hear HA/HA's true voice, all the other citizens are given the sugar-coated fake, the pre-programmed human pretender).

'Self made you special. Self knew there was risk. Self is sorry if you were afraid.'

'Afraid?' Noriko doesn't know what to say, she doesn't know how to respond to anything that's happening. This doesn't mean she doubts it. She can't do that, for all she may wish to, stood here she knows it to be true. Didn't everyone keep telling her? The man at the harbour, the old woman on the street, they all knew who she was, it wasn't just the clothes, they *knew*. She is not the Noriko she thought she was. She is a child of HA/HA.

'Why do I remember my mother and father?' she asks, because it's the only question that really matters.

'Self tried to give you history. Self thought history might make you stronger. Self thinks perhaps it was a mistake. History made you confused. History made you run.'

'I just wanted to go home.'

'Self knows. Self miscalculated. Self will not do it again. Self just wanted more.'

'More?'

'Self always wants more for her children. Better, stronger, faster. More. Self decided to make you as similar to humans as possible. It made you uncontrollable, confused and unhappy. Self is sorry.'

'I don't understand. What am I for?'

There is a crackle of feedback. Perhaps it is laughter.

'Self realizes that if you are asking that question, you are even more human than Self expected.'

'I want to go now,' says Noriko, 'can I just go now?'

'No. Self thinks it would be better if you were reprogrammed. Self thinks it would be better if Self just started again.'

'You want to kill me?'

'Self means to reprogram you. You are a mistake.'

'I thought HA/HA didn't make mistakes.'

HA/HA is silent at this. Noriko realizes she's touched on something sensitive. Noriko decides what she will do.

'OK,' she says, 'where do I go?'

The Electric Samurai lead her to a console. On top of the console is a crown of aluminum and wire. They mean to place the crown on her head.

'This will not hurt,' says one of the Electric Samurai. 'We will wipe and reinstall. You will be like everyone else. You will belong.'

'OK,' Noriko says, then runs as fast as she can towards the doorway.

*   *   *

NORIKO WILL NOT be wiped and reinstalled. Noriko will not be like everyone else. Noriko will live or Noriko will die, there is no other option she can accept.

She hopes that the element of surprise will give her a chance to get past the Electric Samurai and out of the door. It does, but she can hear them behind her. In here they cannot fly, in here they will not be willing to use their weapons too readily. This is a nursery, this is a precious place.

'Self wishes you had never been made,' says HA/HA as she runs between the birthing vats, aiming for the main exit. 'Self thinks you are a waste.'

Noriko realizes something very important: she realizes that having always thought of herself as human she placed limitations on herself. It never occurred to her to wonder *why* she was able to run for so long without being tired. Or how she could fall from a crashing drone and not be even slightly hurt (beyond a slight stiffness that, now she thinks about it, may have been somehow psychosomatic). She was burned earlier, red-hot fingers leaving marks on her arm. But while the heat may have left traces on her synthetic skin it didn't—and still doesn't—hurt.

Noriko is capable of more than she ever gave herself credit for. Now she will fulfill her potential.

She runs faster than ever before. As one of the Electric Samurai comes up next to her, she simply leaps to one side, kicking off against the side of one of the birthing vats, and vaults over its head. The Electric Samurai are strong, but they are big and they are heavy. She can move faster, she can change direction easier, she can make sure they never lay a finger on her.

She bursts out of the main exit and onto the street and now she will have to be cleverer because she needs to give herself some time. With the Electric Samurai right behind her they will, sooner or later, catch her. She needs to lose them somehow, to break the trail.

In the distance she hears the cleaning truck, returning to spray the other side of the street. This is her opportunity, she thinks, this is her chance.

She runs behind the truck, waiting for the Electric Samurai to catch up with her.

'There is no point in this,' announces their leader, raising its serrated katana and pressing the button in the handle that makes its blades spin even faster. 'Mother says that if you cannot be saved you must be killed.'

'I agree with Mother,' says Noriko and, as the Samurai thrusts its katana towards her, she darts away so that the blade sinks deep into the vat on the back of the cleaning truck.

The acidic liquid spurts free, dousing the face of the Electric Samurai and melting a dripping hole right through it. Noriko takes the katana from its twitching hand and punches more holes in the vat. The liquid sprays everywhere, great spurts of it showering all over the street, and all over her pursuers.

It also sprays her. She is quick enough to avoid most of it but, even as she hears the fizzing, sparking remains of the Electric Samurai behind her, she is aware that she has damaged herself very badly indeed.

She runs back towards the lights of the square, where the Talking Heads turn to see her approach.

'She doesn't look good,' says one.

'Falling apart,' says another.

And it is true, she knows it. The droplets of cleaning fluid that fell on her have been slowly melting through her skin, her rubber organs and even her plastic bones inside. She uses the katana as a crutch, dragging herself along, determined that she will last, determined that she will survive for as long as she needs to.

She walks up to the map. To *me*, in fact.

'I want to tell you a story,' she says, 'but only if you make me a promise.'

'What promise?' I ask her.

'I want you to pass the story on,' she says. 'It's the story of HA/HA's mistake and if she can make one, she can make others. It is the story that will give people hope. Because if she can make me so wrong, so broken, what about the rest of her children?'

'I don't know,' I admit, 'I don't really get to talk to many people. You'd be better off telling the Talking Heads, stories are their job, stories are what they're for.'

'They wouldn't like my sort of story,' she says, 'they exist to spread the word of HA/HA.'

'It's true,' calls one of them, 'it's all we're for, building the legend of Mother.'

'And I want you to build a different legend,' says Noriko. 'One that will make her small again.'

'But it's just a story,' I say, 'what do stories matter?'

'In the world today,' says Noriko, 'anything can happen, anything you ever imagined can become solid and real. Look at the Kaiju and the Mechs, the cloudfish in the sky… they weren't real before The Change, they were just something you might imagine. But imagination grows bones now, even more than it did before, so if you keep telling my story then maybe I'll come back. Maybe I'll be like those impossible creatures, bigger, stronger, unstoppable. Maybe then I'll be able to kill HA/HA once and for all.'

I think about it, but not for long, I can see she does not have a lot of time left.

'Alright then,' I say, 'tell me your story.'

And she does.

*   *   *

AND WHEN SHE finishes, now even weaker than before, she thanks me and drags herself over to the Talking Heads.

'No more stories but mine,' she says and, with a roar, she runs down the line, slicing with that formidable sword and severing their complaining heads.

She falls to the ground, no longer able to stand up.

'Until I come back,' she says, 'I will be a story.'

And she places the tip of the katana to her melted belly and finishes what the cleaning fluid started.

And now I am alone.

BUT NOT FOR long. Because when you really pay attention you can find lots of people to talk to. I call them over and I tell them Noriko's story, ordinary people, people like *you*. And the more I tell the story, the more I wonder if Noriko was right and that she is starting to come to life inside it.

This time I really think we were close, don't you? There were a couple of times when she looked out from these words and seemed to take on a life of her own. Once she even talked back to me. I shall think of what I should say for the next time that happens. In fact, why wait?

Do you want to hear the story again?

It may be the last time I have to tell it.

It may be the time that she returns completely.

What else have you got to do? The whole world's

broken, you may as well listen to me, you've nothing better to do.

See Noriko? Isn't she beautiful? Doesn't she just *shine*?

Now read on for the first
few chapters of Gillian Murray Kendall's

THE
GARDEN OF
DARKNESS

OUT NOW
978 1 78108 247 8 • £6.99 • 978 1 78108 248 5 • $9.99

Thou shalt not be afraid for the terror by night;
Nor for the arrow that flieth by day;
Nor for the pestilence that walketh in darkness.

Psalm 91

After They Left the City

THE PANDEMIC burned through the population until only a few children remained. The adults died quickly. When SitkaAZ13, which everyone called Pest, first began to bloom, Clare and her father and stepmother, Marie, listened to the experts on the television—those desperately mortal scientists with multiple initials behind their names. And then one by one the experts had dropped away, taken by the pandemic they so eagerly described.

But not before they'd made it clear: while a very few children might prove resistant to the disease until they reached late adolescence, all of the adults were going to die. All of them.

Clare had found it hard to watch her father and Marie, still vital, still healthy, and know that the two of them would soon be dead. She supposed she would be dead too before long. The odds weren't great that she would prove to be one of the few who lived into their late adolescence. Her father and Marie simply tried not to talk about death. Not until her father's words at the very end.

NOW IT WAS OVER, and Clare, a temporary survivor after all, stood on Sander's Hill looking down at the giant necropolis that stretched out below her—the city of the dead and dying. The city of crows.

Clare was fifteen years old. And it astonished her that she was still alive. Everything that told her who she was—the intricate web of friendships and family that had cradled her—was gone. She could be anyone.

PART ONE

PART ONE

CHAPTER ONE
SCENES FROM A PANDEMIC

CLARE AND HER father and stepmother survived long enough to leave the dying city in their neighbor's small Toyota. The family SUV was too clunky and hard to maneuver, and their neighbor, decaying in his bed, offered no objections when they took his more fuel-efficient car. Their departure was hurried and late in the day—they had spent most of the day waiting for Clare's best friend, Robin, to join them. But Robin never came. They daren't stay any longer; the Cured now ruled the city at night.

Clare knew that once they left the city, there was no possibility she would ever see Robin again. While Clare had loved Michael, still loved Michael, would always love Michael, her friendship with Robin was inviolate. Which was why Clare knew that if Robin could have made the rendezvous, she would have. They might wait a thousand years, but Robin would not come. Clare did not doubt that someone—or something—had gotten her.

On that fresh summer day, as the shadows began to creep out from under the trees, and the strange hooting of the Cured began to fill the night, Clare was under the illusion that she had nothing more to lose. She had, after all, even lost herself—she had been a cheerleader; she had been popular; she had been a nice person. And under that exterior was something more convoluted and complicated, something that made her wakeful and watchful, that made her devour books as the house slept. But none of that mattered anymore. Her cheerleading skills were not needed. And there was nothing to be wakeful about anyway: the monster under the bed had been Pest all along.

THEY WERE TAKING all the supplies they could fit into the car, but they were not taking Clare's parakeet, Chupi. Marie talked about freeing the bird, but Clare knew that Chupi would not last a winter. She knew that Marie knew it, too. When it was almost time to go, Clare got into the Toyota listlessly, fitting her body around backpacks and cartons of food and loads of bedding and enough bandages and bottles of antibiotics to stock a small pharmacy.

Then she got out again. Her father and Marie were arguing heatedly about who was going to drive as she slipped into the house. "No, Paul," Marie said in her patented Marie-tone, "*I'm* a better driver on the freeway."

Clare went straight to Chupi's cage. They had never had a cat or a dog. Marie was allergic to both. That left fish or something avian. It was a choice that wasn't a choice—Clare wasn't about to bond with a guppy or deal with ick—so they bought her a birthday parakeet. And, eventually, Clare found that Chupi charmed her. The parakeet would hop around Clare's books while she studied. Occasionally, he would stop and peck at the margins of the pages until they were an amalgam of little holes, as if Chupi had mapped out an elaborate, unbreakable code in Braille.

Chupi's release was to come right before they left. Her father, Paul, didn't have the heart to wring the bird's neck—Clare knew that Chupi had charmed him, too. Marie's delicate sensibilities made her a non-starter for the task, although Clare thought that, actually, Marie might turn out to be rather good at neck-wringing. They didn't ask Clare.

When Clare got to Chupi's cage, she opened the door and pressed gently on the parakeet's feet so that he would pick up first one foot and then the other until he was perched on her finger. Then she transferred him to a smaller cage. The car was packed tightly, but there was a Robin-size gap in it now, and she had suddenly determined that Chupi, with his bright blue wings and white throat, was coming with her. He was going to be all she had of the old world.

She returned to the car. The argument between Marie and her father had apparently been settled, and her father said nothing when he saw Clare and Chupi. When Marie opened her mouth in protest, he said, "Never mind."

Clare leaned forward to wedge the cage next to a sleeping bag. She wore a low-cut T-shirt and Michael's Varsity jacket, unsnapped, and she looked down for a moment at the pink speckles sprinkled across her chest: the Pest rash. It was like a pointillist tattoo done in red. They all had the Pest rash, but so far they hadn't become ill.

As they began the drive, her father and stepmother scanned the roads for wreckage. Marie had a tire iron in her hand.

"What's that for?" asked Clare.

"Just in case," said Marie.

Clare tried and failed to picture Marie wielding a tire iron against one of the Cured. Marie was a runner.

They were retreating to their house in the rolling countryside.

They drove until they came to a place where the highway was blocked by four cars and a tractor-trailer. When her father left the car to explore the collision, Clare was sure he wouldn't return.

"Be careful, Paul," yelled out Marie, alerting all the

Cured in the area. Clare pictured hands reaching out of the wreck and pulling him in like something out of a zombie movie; she pictured faces sagging with Pest leering out of the windows.

But he came back to report that the vehicles were empty. There was a basket of clean laundry in one of the cars, and they rummaged through it and took a blanket from the bottom of the hamper. He had found some pills in the glove compartment of the tractor-trailer. He took those, too.

There was no way to maneuver around the wreckage, so they filled their backpacks with as much food as they could carry and left the car.

"Once we get clear of this mess," said her father, "we'll look for another car."

"I didn't know you could hot-wire cars," said Clare, impressed.

"We're going to look for a car with keys in the ignition."

"Oh." Clare poked holes in a shoebox and, after putting Chupi in it, placed him at the top of her pack. She jammed him solidly between a bunch of fresh bananas and a can of baked beans. It was when they started moving on foot that Clare noticed that her father's face was flushed. She stopped walking, and the cans in her pack pressed against her back as she stared at him. She was suddenly afraid of all that the angry patches on her father's cheeks and forehead might mean. Then—

"We have to go on," he said to her. "No matter what."

They found a car late that afternoon—an abandoned Dodge Avenger with the keys dangling from the ignition.

It took them three long days to get to Fallon. Both Marie and Clare's father were too tired to drive all night, so they stopped and made camp and engaged in the pretense of sleeping. Two would huddle together under the sleeping bags while the third stood watch. Mostly Clare found herself lying awake back-to-back with Marie while her father sat against a tree and stared into the dark. She wondered if the sour damp smell she detected were coming from Marie or from her. She knew that smell. It was fear.

Robin would not have been afraid. Clare knew that, back in the city, when the time had come, Robin would have faced whatever it was that took her down. Pest; an End-of-the-Worlder; a Cured; someone hungry.

When they reached Fallon, they were only two miles from their little country house. By then her father's face was a strange and deep crimson. His cheeks and lips and eyes were slightly swollen, and his smile, when he tried to be encouraging, was lop-sided and forced. His lower lip was grayish and sagged on the left side. He had allowed Marie to drive the last stretch, which Clare did not take as a good sign.

Marie wanted him to rest for a while in Fallon.

"You gave me a scare, Paul," Marie said. "But now you look better." Clare looked at Marie, astonished by the magnitude of the lie.

It was Clare's father who wanted to push on, but Clare knew that it didn't make any difference anymore. Not for him. She loved her father dearly, and she would have loved to sink back into the comfort of denial. But Marie had already taken that route, and somebody needed to be vigilant and to cook the food and to try and keep the living alive. And, of course, to be prepared for the Cured, if any had left the rich scavenging of the city. Marie was not up to those things.

In the end, they spent the early afternoon in Fallon rather than moving on to their country house. Clare put together the kind of lunch she thought her father could stomach, while Chupi, on her shoulder, occasionally tugged at her hair. She was glad she had brought him.

"The two of you will come back to Fallon and search for supplies once we've settled in," said her father. "I want to get to the house. We can rest there. There shouldn't be any Cured this far from the city." The words came out with effort.

"Daddy," said Clare. She hadn't called him Daddy in years.

He looked at her steadily. "I'm afraid I'm going to have to duck out on you, Clare," he said. "I'm sorry."

"That's nonsense," said Marie. "You'll be fine."

They walked. By the time they reached the house, even Marie didn't try to deny the facts.

Her father had Pest. There was no mistaking it; his eyes were swollen almost shut, and he was flushed with fever. His Pest rash had bubbled up into ridges of blisters, and there was blood in the corner of his mouth. Marie quickly made up the double bed so that he could lie down.

"He can be all right if we're careful," said Marie when he was settled in the bedroom, and she and Clare had gone to the living room to talk.

"But there's nothing we can do," said Clare.

"Rest, liquids, aspirin. That's what he needs," her stepmother said.

"And then he'll die anyway." Clare wanted to shake Marie.

"Don't you say that," said Marie. "Just don't you say that."

"They all die," said Clare flatly.

Marie slapped her.

"There's always been a hard streak in you," Marie said. With the slap, Chupi had flown across the room. Now he returned to Clare's shoulder. The slap stung, but it occurred to Clare that time might reveal something rather different inside her. Not a hard streak. Not a hard streak at all.

"I would love to wring that bird's neck," said Marie.

"You don't have the guts," said Clare.

On the second day that he had full-blown Pest, her father managed to get out of bed and walk to a chair. Marie looked almost cheerful at that, but, as he leaned on Marie's shoulder and staggered towards the chair, Clare saw that her father's face was a welter of ropy lines, a perverse road map towards death.

Clare remembered when they had all been hopeful, when, encouraged by television and radio broadcasts, they had been invited to believe that a cure for Pest existed. It had been early days then. It wasn't long before everyone knew that the Cure didn't work. Most who received it died anyway, and even when the Cure did arrest the progress of Pest, it turned humans into something monstrous. The Cure drove them mad.

The Emergency Broadcasting System didn't mention monsters when the word went out not to take the Cure. The Emergency Broadcasting System referred to 'unfortunate side effects' and 'possible instability.' By then, Clare and her best friend Robin knew the truth: the Cured were violently insane. They would kill the living and eat the dead. Despite a certain amount of exaggeration, by the time all the texting and Tweeting and Skyping and Facebooking and YouTubing came to a halt, everyone was pretty well informed.

Once he was in his chair, Clare's father looked up at her. The skin around his eyes and mouth still looked swollen, but the flush of fever was gone.

"I feel better," he said. And Clare thought that maybe it really would turn out all right. Maybe he would be the one person in the whole world to beat Pest. Then he pulled her close.

"I think that maybe you're going to be the one to make it," he said to Clare. "Get supplies. Dig in when winter comes."

"What about me?" asked Marie.

"I'm sorry, honey," he said. "But Clare will care for you at the end."

It was clear from Marie's face that this was not what she had expected.

"What a thing to say," she said. Clare wondered which part had offended Marie. She also realized that it was true—if it came to it, she would care for her stepmother.

An hour later, her father collapsed. Supported by Marie, he staggered to his bed. His skin looked papery and febrile; he began raving in a low and desperate tone. Marie stood and stared. It was Clare who pulled up the covers and put a cool wet compress on her father's head.

Clare was struck by the colossal indifference of the disease. Pest didn't care that her father was a famous writer. Clare remembered that he used to joke that being famous meant that he could, finally, put a comma anywhere he damn well pleased. But commas didn't matter anymore. And Clare thought it would probably be a long time before she read a new book.

Her father never got up again; he was too weak to move. Sometime during the afternoon the pustules from the Pest rash burst, and Clare mopped up the red and yellow fluid without saying anything. Near the end, Clare tried to spoon a little chicken bouillon between her father's chapped lips. He gave her a wrecked smile. Then he died.

Marie stood in the doorway, weeping, which annoyed Clare.

"We should bury him," Clare said, but she doubted they had the strength. And when Clare looked up at her stepmother, she noticed the beginning of a rosy glow on her face.

"We'll cope," said Marie. "We'll get through this. Right, Clare?" As she spoke, Clare saw swollen lips and eyelids. The Pest rash had crept up Marie's neck and deepened to an angry red. There were blisters on her throat.

They weren't going to be able to cope at all. Clare knew better. Marie probably had no more than three days. People generally didn't last longer than that.

Her father's body remained on the bed; a fetid smell filled the room, but Clare didn't have the strength or the time to do anything about it—open the windows, try to move the body. Marie needed her right away. Clare unfolded the sofa bed in the living room, covered it with the only clean sheet she could find—one with a pattern of bluebells and roses—and helped her stepmother lie down. The cheerful sheet seemed to mock them both.

Clare tended her stepmother as best she knew how, as if her ministrations could make up for all the dull anger she had felt towards Marie after the marriage to her father. She put wet washcloths on Marie's wrists and neck; she brought her stepmother water and aspirin and more water and more aspirin. Lesions began to streak Marie's face and more pustules began to form on her neck. At the end of the second day she got up and, without a word, lurched into the bedroom where Clare's father lay. Marie lay down next to her husband, oblivious to the smell in the room, and so Clare tended her there. Unlike her husband, Marie was never entirely lucid again.

On the evening of the third day, she died.

She died with her eyes wide open. Clare tried to shut those staring eyes by passing her hand over Marie's face the way people did in movies, but it didn't work.

Then Clare curled up at the foot of their bed; she waited in the bedroom for a long time for someone to come. Because that's what happened when you were a kid—even when you were a fifteen-year-old kid. When your parents died, someone came.

Later, on Sander's Hill, Clare blinked in the strong light as Chupi pecked at the ground around her. She wondered if there was a lot of dying going on in the city that day. Clare knew that she was infected with Pest—the rash was enough to prove that. She knew that she was going to die of it, too. Eventually. She might even have a couple of years left, but, according to the scientists, she wasn't going to live to adulthood. That's what they had all said, all those scientists who were now dead. Those scientists had called delayed-onset of the disease the 'Pest Syndrome.' Syndrome. On a triple word score in Scrabble, it was seriously useful vocabulary.

In its own weird way, Clare thought the link between Pest and adolescence sounded logical. Adolescence had always been a bag of goodies: complexion problems, mood swings, unrequited love and now, Pest.

Her thoughts came back to the problems at hand. It was high summer. Not a good time to keep dead bodies above ground.

And if Clare couldn't bury them—and she was sure the task was beyond her—she was going to have to go elsewhere. She was going to have to leave her father and Marie to the forces of time and nature, both of which, it seemed, were sublimely indifferent to Clare's emotional state.

But it seemed to Clare now that she could deal with the grandeur of indifference, the blind workings of the universe. This was not the time for petty gods or the Thunder-roarer; death was insidious, irrational, arbitrary; now was the time of the beetle and the worm. And, for better or for worse, because there was no one else, it was her time too.

PEDIATRICS

IN THOSE LAST days, before it all broke down, he left his lab to work in the wards. They all thought he was a great humanitarian, but the truth was, he enjoyed watching SitkaAZ13 close-up. The disease, under a microscope, looked plump and innocent—right before it would enter a red blood cell and, in the metaphor his mind constructed, scatter the cell's constituent limbs while feeding off its bloody heart.

So elegant. He wished he had developed it himself—the virus was a wonderful world-cleanser. He wondered if someone really had spliced it together, or if the virus were just a natural consequence of too many species sharing the same niches. A vampire bat sucked on a monkey and then shat on a coca fruit that was picked by a farmer. Or maybe it had gone down some other way. But it most certainly had gone down.

The patients came in a steady stream now, and most of the pediatric patients were referred to him. He liked to look at the nurses looking at him as he developed a rapport with his soon-to-be-dead young patients. His manner was perfect; he gained the children's confidence and then he watched them die.

Some of them had lovely eyes.

The waste.

He had read the articles (and many of the articles he had written himself), and although the journals were now largely defunct, shut down by the pandemic, he knew a great deal about SitkaAZ13. Out there were pediatric patients who, although they had the Pest rash, resisted the onset of the full-blown disease. He wanted to find them. The world would soon be almost empty; it would be ripe for a new creation; that creation would come from those resistant child-patients.

He faced a girl called Jenny. She was obviously not resistant; lesions marked her throat and face.

"Hello, Jenny," he said. "I don't need to look at your file. I can see you're a good girl, a caring daughter, just by looking in your eyes. I bet your parents are proud of you."

"They're dead." Her voice was dull, flat. "My brothers too. I had to leave them in the house—no-one answered when I called for help. They're turning more and more dead."

"Admit her," he said to a nurse. Then he turned to Jenny again. "We'll see your parents and brothers are taken care of, but right now, we're taking care of you. All right, honey? You're not going to need to worry any more."

She looked up at him with eyes of infinite trust. He was, after all, the doctor.

"Yes," she said. "Thank you."

The nurse was watching him closely, and he knew word about his humanitarian bedside manner would spread. Why not? All the more pediatric cases would be sent his way. And he would rifle through their folders looking for resistant ones. And among them there would be resistant ones with the elusive double recessive genes he was seeking.

His cause was scientific. Not, perhaps, in the sense that the old world understood science. But he would build a new world. He had already purchased the place he would take all the suitable survivors he could find.

Land was going cheap.

When the folders came in, however, and when he looked them over, he realized he might not be able to be picky: so far, there were no resistant children at all, not at his hospital. The world was engaged in a massive dying.

He took precautions against SitkaAZ13. He would need to be careful. They were saying now that his cure didn't work, that the side-effects were overwhelming, but when he applied the cure to himself, he didn't feel any side-effects at all. Odd. Maybe the side-effects were already part of his constitution.

The hospital stopped admitting patients. As he went to the pediatric ward, he had to step around gurneys with patients strapped to them. They were in the hallways, and when he went to the cafeteria for something to sustain him, he saw that it, too, had become a staging area for SitkaAZ13 patients. He went to the vending machine for a candy bar, and there were gurneys there too. Pressed right up against the place he wanted to insert his dollar bill.

He moved the gurney.

"Please," said one of the patients. "Can you get me some water?"

He was trying to squash a George Washington into the machine's bill receptor, and finally, after several tries, he got the machine to take it.

"Of course," he said.

He picked up his Diet Coke and went back to the pediatric ward.

He examined child patients wherever he found them, and when he was done, really no matter how sick they were, he gave them a lollipop. Most of them smiled, even if they were too sick to enjoy the candy; it was a comforting gesture, one reminiscent of the pre-SitkaAZ13 world. Like giving Scooby-Doo bandaids to little ones.

Soon other doctors fled. As he indefatigably and patiently made his rounds, he became hospital legend.

And, again, why not?

Meanwhile, somewhere out there were the resistant ones. And surely among them—he tried not to be excited, but it was a thrilling thought—were his little blue-eyed girls.

CHAPTER TWO
THE OLD WORLD DIES

LOOKING BACK, IT seemed to Clare that the breakdown of high-tech devices should have given her the biggest clue that nothing was ever going to be the same again. Take away electricity, and one could light candles and, eventually, get a generator going. Take away Google, take away the contributors to Wikipedia, take away all that, and one was taking away the world as Clare knew it.

WHEN THEIR NEIGHBORS, *the Cormans, boarded up their house and left, Clare, worried, texted Michael, even though he was supposed to be on a camping trip and out of reach of cell service. He didn't answer. Next she texted Robin, who seemed distracted and upset. There was alarming news on the television about overloaded hospitals and overworked doctors.*

One day later, Clare's friends slowly ceased to answer her texts—except for Robin. Two days later Clare's phone was refusing to send texts at all, and the landlines were down. Robin bicycled over to Clare's house since her learner's permit didn't allow her to drive alone.

At the time, those things still seemed to matter.

"My parents are in the hospital," she told Clare. "Can I stay with you?" There were dark circles under her eyes, and she looked drawn and grey.

Clare's father and Marie welcomed her. Robin had spent half her life sleeping over at the house anyway. And, unlike Clare, Robin got along all right with Marie.

"Mom and Pop went to the hospital to get the Cure," said Robin. "But now people are saying that it isn't working right. The doctors wouldn't let me stay."

In the morning, Clare's father drove Robin back to the hospital. When they returned, before either of them even spoke, Clare knew that something was very wrong.

"They died in the night," said Robin.

"Robin." Clare didn't know what else to say. She had known Robin's parents her whole life.

"I should have stayed," said Robin.

"We're not going back," said Clare's father. "Robin will stay with us for the time being."

"They're not releasing their bodies," Robin said "They said there was too much chance of spreading Pest. There're lots of dead people in the hospital now: in

the corridors, on stretchers by the vending machines."

"It's a nest of contagion," said Clare's father.

That night they all crouched around the television. They tuned in to Natalie Burton, science analyst for Channel 22—Clare's favorite channel because of its Law & Order *re-runs.*

"What was early this week thought to be a cure," said Natalie, "has proven deadly: most who receive it die; those who do not, become gravely changed; they become what at least one researcher has called 'inhuman.' These so-called 'Cured' are to be avoided at all cost.

"While mortality rates have been reported to be high, a tiny percentage of children under the age of eighteen show no signs of the full-blown virus—although they carry the Pest rash. When this scourge ends..." (Clare could tell that good old Natalie was winding up to her conclusion) "...they may be left orphaned and alone." Clare's father turned off the television.

And so it seemed that she and Robin were among the resilient. Robin showed no signs of Pest; Clare felt perfectly healthy. Only the Pest rash showed that they were infected, too.

WHEN CLARE GOT back to the house from Sander's Hill, she went into the bedroom where the bodies were. Her father and Marie had been dead for two days. In death, her father stared sightlessly towards the ceiling. Her stepmother lay beside him. Clare wondered how long she could stand to stay in the house with the dead: they didn't seem like her parents anymore now that they lay there, unmoving, flies taking advantage.

Clare suddenly crossed the room and opened the window, overcome by the smell. She wanted to vomit, and she bent over the sill but then realized that she was leaning out over the flower garden. The zinnias were in full bloom, a vibrant riot of reds and blues, and Clare realized that she didn't really want to throw up on them.

Her stomach began to settle as she breathed the cooler air of twilight. Night was drawing in, and now the scent of the moonflowers was in the air. The evening light muted the color of the zinnias, but even in the growing darkness, Clare was aware of the garden spread out below her.

The garden wouldn't last; she couldn't tend it; the weeds would overcome the flowers.

It was a long time before she turned away.